ABDO Publishing Company is the exclusive school and library distributor of Rabbit Ears Books.

Library bound edition 2005.

Library of Congress Cataloging-in-Publication Data

Kunstler, James Howard.
  Davy Crockett / James Howard Kunstler ; illustrated by Steve Brodner.
    p. cm.
  "Rabbit Ears books."
  ISBN 1-59197-762-2
    1. Crockett, Davy, 1786-1836—Juvenile literature. 2.
Pioneers—Tennessee—Biography—Juvenile literature. 3. Tennessee—Biography—Juvenile
literature. 4. Legislators—United States—Biography—Juvenile literature. 5. United States.
Congress. House—Biography—Juvenile literature. [1. Crockett, Davy, 1786-1836. 2.
Pioneers. 3. Legislators.] I. Brodner, Steve, ill. II. Title.

F436.C95K86 2005
976.8'04'092—dc22
[B]

                                                                    2004046999

All Rabbit Ears books are reinforced library binding
and manufactured in the United States of America.

JAMES HOWARD KUNSTLER

Davy Crockett

Illustrated by

STEVE BRODNER

RABBIT EARS BOOKS

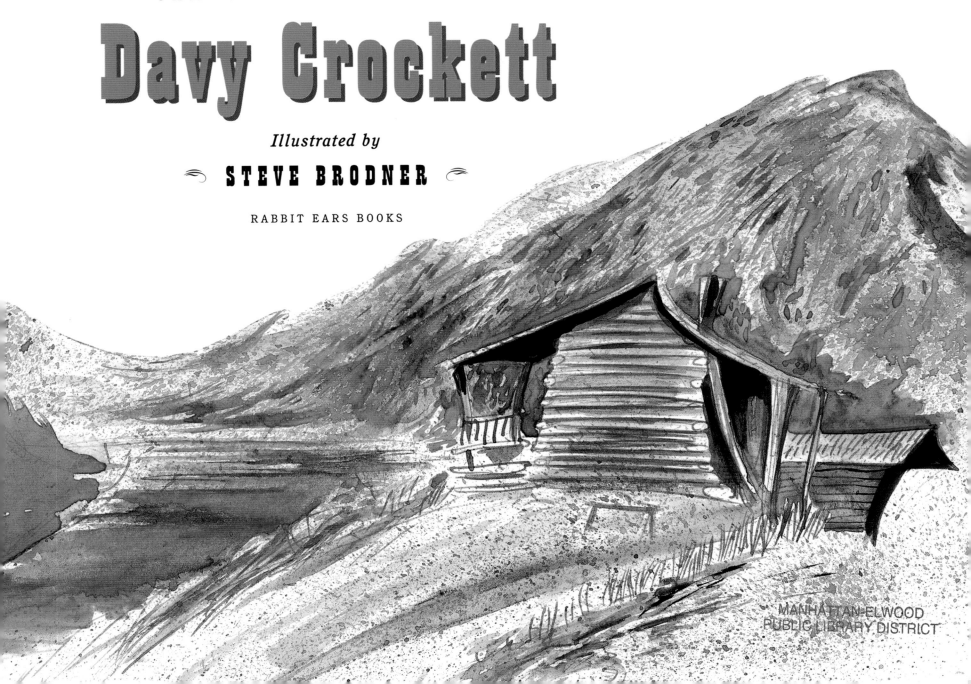

My name is Davy Crockett and I am a legend of American history. The original ring-tailed roarer of the western woods, I call myself. The yellow blossom of the gum swamp. Whoo-hee! I was a beauty. 'Course, I was a flesh and blood person: born and lived and loved my wife and babies. Then I passed into the celestial vapors from where I speak. Young folks ought to know their history, and how a person gets to be a legend. So these here are the naked, green-skinned facts of my life, and a lot of it is the truth, too.

I was born when this land was young, on a river called the Nolachucky, in a wild part of the republic called Tennessee, before they even made it a state. How wild was it? Well, it was so full of bears that they set up a bear legislature and you couldn't chop down a tree without bears climbing the stump to give a speech. It was so wild that the only human folks they let in were Crocketts, because a Crockett can grin any wild varmint out of countenance.

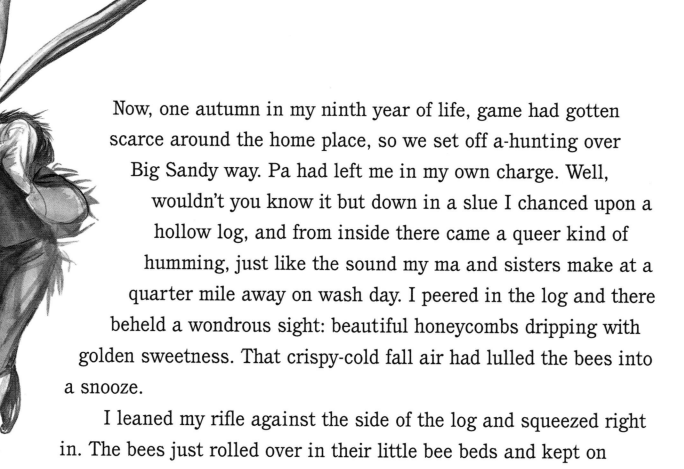

Now, one autumn in my ninth year of life, game had gotten scarce around the home place, so we set off a-hunting over Big Sandy way. Pa had left me in my own charge. Well, wouldn't you know it but down in a slue I chanced upon a hollow log, and from inside there came a queer kind of humming, just like the sound my ma and sisters make at a quarter mile away on wash day. I peered in the log and there beheld a wondrous sight: beautiful honeycombs dripping with golden sweetness. That crispy-cold fall air had lulled the bees into a snooze.

I leaned my rifle against the side of the log and squeezed right in. The bees just rolled over in their little bee beds and kept on a-humming while I partook of a honey feast.

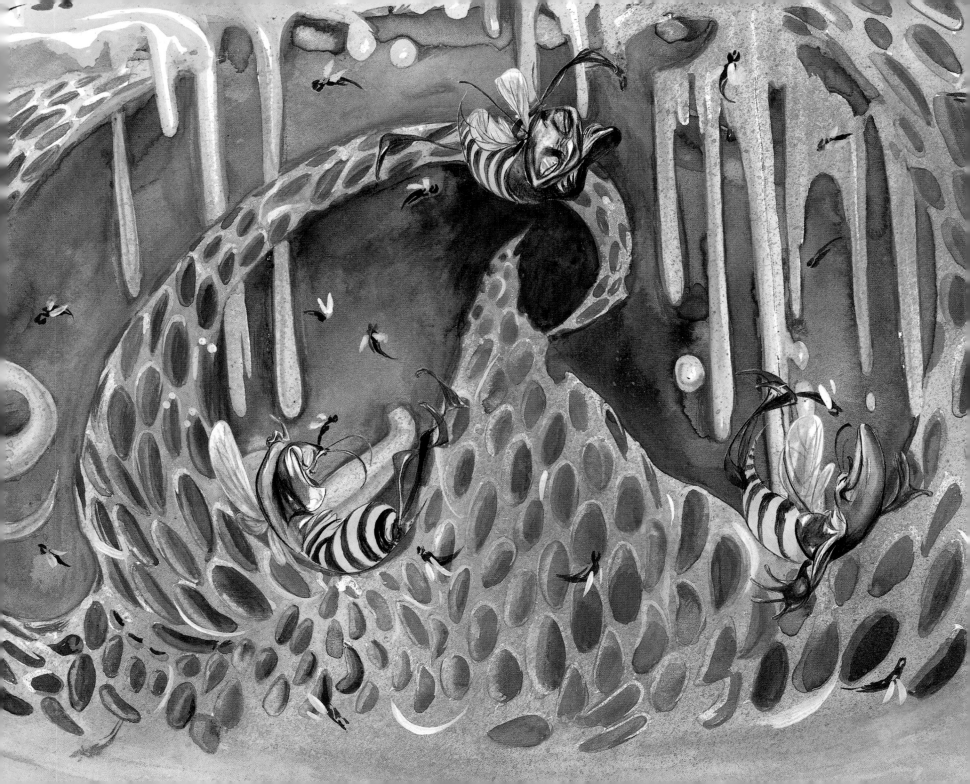

By and by, I felt something poking my posterities, like the cold snout of a dog.

"Get back now, old Thunder!" said I, a-thinking it was Pa's best hound.

But all I heard was a low growl, *Grrrrr,* and then more poking from behind until my face was shoved up into that sticky old mess of honeycomb.

"By the Great Horn Spoon!" I said to myself, understanding all of a sudden that I was between a bear and his noonday meal.

Meantime, snug as we all were, it was warming up in that old hollow log. Those bees had woken up from their slumber. *"Bzzzzzzzz!"* said the bees.

Now, in such a fix I had to ask myself which I preferred: a face full of bees or a face full of bear. And finally I reckoned that I might find fairer use for my face on the bear end of things, and vice-versa my posteriors at the bee end. So I sqwoonched about and squoze around until I was a-staring that lumbering varmint snout to snout.

"Why, how d'you do, stranger?" said I, hoping to establish respectful terms right off. "Ain't it a fine day, though?"

"*Grrrrr,*" said the bear.

"Why, you are right about that," said I. "And there is nothing on this earth that beats a honey lunch. I can avouch it, 'cause I've just eaten one here in this very log, and there is plenty left. Let others have their blood-soaked viands, their 'possum innards, their livers and gizzards. Give me sweet, fresh honey every time."

"*Grrrrr,*" said the bear.

Well, by now those bees had warmed themselves to full alertness and, noticing how I had chawed a pretty good portion of their honeycomb, they began to abuse my posteriors with their stingers. It was all I could do not to holler and moan. But I just put on my finest two-dollar grin and said to the bear:

"If you let me crawl out of this here hollow log, kind stranger, you will find a clear path to the fattest honeycombs this side of Sunday."

"*Bzzzzzzz, Bzzzzzzz!*" said the bees.

"But if you decide to chaw my head off instead, why then my frozen carcass will plug up the log, and you'll have to wait until spring to have your treat."

"*Hmmmmmmmm,*" said the bear.

Apparently he was a-studying the matter. All the while those bees used my straggling hams for target practice, and it felt like my pants were peppered with bird shot.

"Make up your goshdurn mind, stranger," I cussed that bear. "Chaw my head off, or let me pass!"

Wouldn't you know he slid out. And I crawled none too gingerly to the opening, my hindermost quarters nearly aflame with bee stings.

"Stand fast now," I told that bear.

I guess his civility had found itself at last, for he did as I asked, and was all smiles about it, too. But no sooner did I pop my swollen posteriors from that hollow gum log, like a cork from a jug, than the swarm of bees busted out. Angry is not the word to describe their frame of mind—they were out for scalps. And seeing that hulking figure of a bear, they at once beset the poor critter like a thunderstorm a-swarming over the peak of Old Baldy, and both bear and bees lit out of the slue like lightning. I never did see that particular bear again, though I knew many more like him.

Well, by and by I grew up and married pretty Polly Finley, and together we had a mess of daughters. But the hunting grew scarcer and so we moved to the Elk River country further west. They called it the Shakes, because the earthquake of 1811 struck hard there.

One fine afternoon at the place called Tims Ford, I came across an old tom 'possum peacefully sunning himself amidst a glade of prickly ash. I clapped the breech of Brown Betsy directly to my shoulder, and would have sent a charge of lead a-whistling his way, but he lifted up a paw and stopped me from firing.

"Is y-y-your name C-c-crockett?" he asked.

"Why, burn my britches if I am not Davy Crockett to the very bone," said I.

"Then, you needn't take any further trouble, for I consider myself as good as shot," the 'possum said. And at once he waddled out of the prickly ash, declaring, "Show me your skillet and I shall jump right in it."

I stooped down to pat the little varmint's noggin. "May I be skinned myself before I harm a hair on your head," said I, "for I never had such a compliment in all my days. Get along now and live a good clean 'possum life."

Off he waddled, with my blessing.

Well, it was along about that same year that General Andy Jackson recruited us to fight the Red Sticks down Alabamy way after they burnt down Fort Mims. I went, and "Old Hickory," as they called Jackson, made me a colonel. But I saw much that disgusted me in that war, and I never did hold with chasing tribes from their rightful lands in a cheating way. It put me and General Jackson at a permanent variance, and when I came home from the war, I got into politics.

By then, Tennessee had become a state. Human beings came to edge out bears, so my
neighbors asked me
to run for Congress.
I reckoned I had
learned enough about
stump-speaking from
the bears to go ahead
and electioneer, so
I did. But votes
were precious
scarce in the
district and
I had to
hunt
'em
up
every
which
way I
could.

So another time I was riding a
broadhorn down the Mississippi
when I came across a fellow floating
downstream in the stern of his keelboat
fast asleep with a jug between his legs.
"Hallo, stranger!" I hollered out a warning.
"Wake up now before she runs away on you!"
He didn't stir a whisker, so as I floated
past, I gave him a jab with my steering oar.
"Whoa!" he said, a-coming to life. "Who
asked you to scratch my lice?"

"You're a-heading straight for
snags," I informed him.

"Shut up before your teeth get
sunburnt," he said, looking up all
squinty-eyed. "I don't value you more
than a chaw of plug tobacky."

"What!" said I, growing wolfy at
his impudence. "Come ashore then and I
shall give you a severe licking!"

He ran his boat plumb into shore. I followed on the broadhorn. Wouldn't you know that eight more brawny fellows climbed out of his cabin and sprang to shore.

"Who are these?" I asked.

"Why, these here are my twin brothers," he said, "and we always fight as one."

I had never seen such a mess of twins before, and it made me eight times as wolfy, so we went straight to the licking. They were right smart varmints, too, but I gave them a frightful beating in

reverse size order until they cried "Stop!" at each note of the scale.

"You are a rip-staver!" the oldest twin declared. "If I knew your name, I'd vote for you in the election."

"It's Crockett," said I, "and I am standing for Congress in this very district."

"Why, then, my brothers and I shall cast as many ballots for you as they will allow," he said, and we all parted fast friends.

Well, I was elected and served three terms in Washington, but I ran head on into my old adversary, Andy Jackson, who had become president by then. We butted horns at every turn: on cheap lands for the western squatters; on breaking treaties we signed with the Cherokee. Politics was sad work. Finally, they spent twenty-five dollars a vote to defeat me in the election.

"Congress can go to perdition!" I roared. "I'm a-going to Texas."

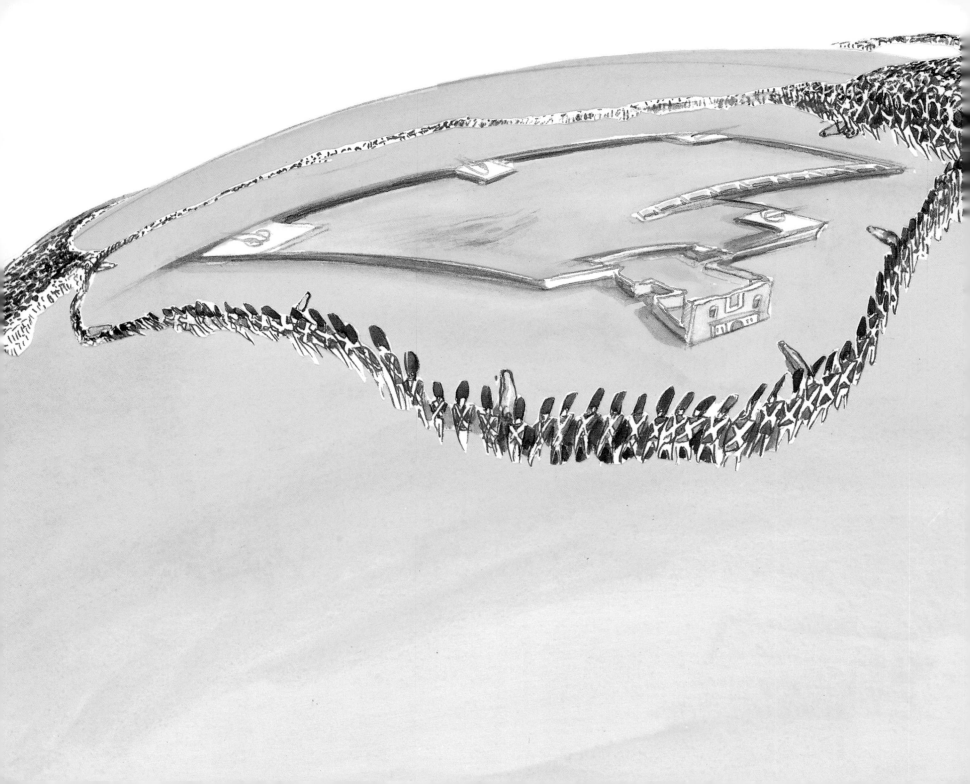

Now, at the time, Texas was still owned by Mexico. 'Course, for years the Mexican government had invited Americans to settle up Texas, so as to tame it for 'em. They said, "Here's a thousand acres each, Señor Yankee Doodle! Come on down and be a part of this here country." And settle they did. It was a garden spot. I had great hopes of making my family's fortune there.

By and by, the Americans said, "Why, there's enough of us here to start a government of our own. We'll call it the Republic of Texas." The Mexicans didn't like that. They fixed to run this rebellion into a gopher hole. That's how I came to be at the Alamo. The Alamo was an old Spanish church down in San Antonio de Bexar that the Mexicans used as a fort. Well, the Texans had come and pitched 'em out. The Mexicans didn't like that, either, and they sent a whole army to swap it back.

The Texans cried out for help. I showed up with twelve Tennessee volunteers none too soon. There were less than two hundred of us in all. General Santa Anna had almost seven thousand troops camped close by on the Medina River.

Our commander was the gallant Colonel William Travis. The enemy sent a message asking for his surrender, and he answered with a cannon shot. They kept us buttoned up in that old Alamo for thirteen days, hurling cannon shot at the walls night and day, but we did not lose a man. Before long, we defenders of the Alamo were living on nothing but pure hope.

Trying to keep spirits up, I climbed right on top of the ramparts, and flapped my arms, and crowed like a rooster. "Cock-a-doodle-doo!" I hollered. "I am half alligator, half horse,

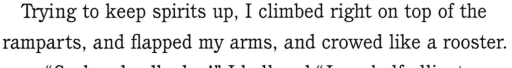

and half snapping turtle, with a touch of earthquake thrown in! I have got the closest shooting rifle, the ugliest coon dog, the roughest racking horse, and the prettiest wife in the state of Tennessee! I can whip my weight in wildcats, ride a streak of lightning through your crab apple patch, put a rifle ball between the horns of the moon, and outstare all the Frenchmen in New Orleans! I can run faster, squat lower, dive deeper, stay under longer, and come out drier than any man this side of the Big Muddy!"

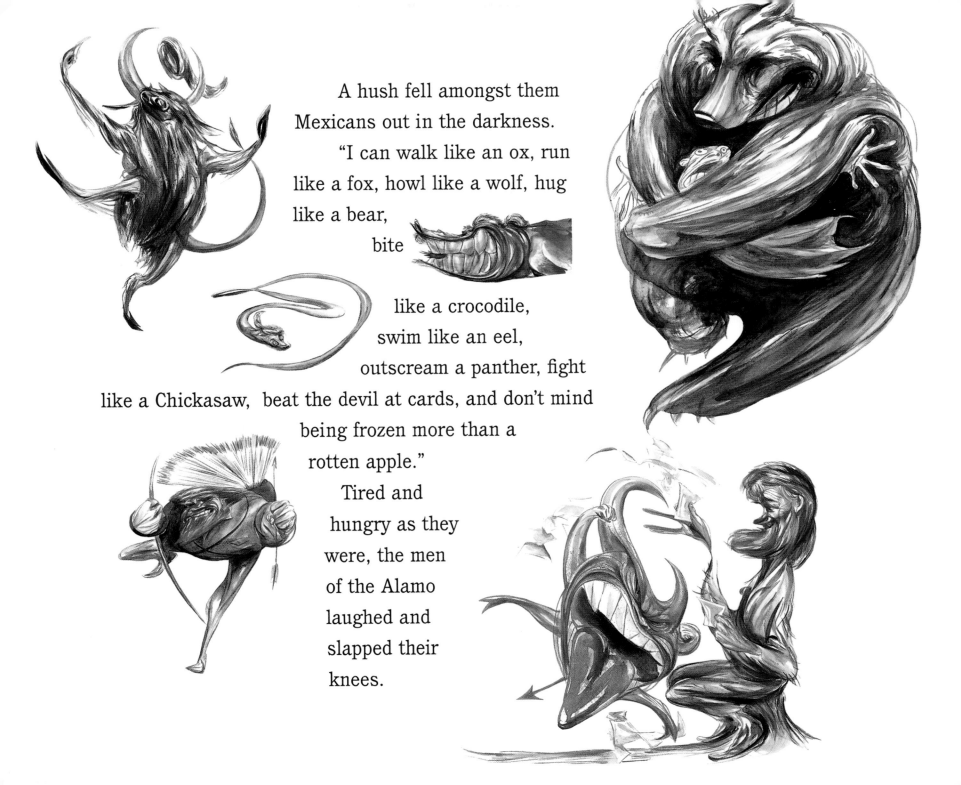

A hush fell amongst them
Mexicans out in the darkness.

"I can walk like an ox, run
like a fox, howl like a wolf, hug
like a bear,
bite
like a crocodile,
swim like an eel,
outscream a panther, fight
like a Chickasaw, beat the devil at cards, and don't mind
being frozen more than a
rotten apple."

Tired and
hungry as they
were, the men
of the Alamo
laughed and
slapped their
knees.

"I can grin a hurricane out of countenance, recite the Bible from Genesee to Christmas, blow the wind of liberty through a squash vine, tote a steamboat on my back, frighten the old folks, suck forty rattlesnake eggs at one sitting, and swallow General Santy Anna whole without choking, if you butter his head and pin his ears back!"

The boys on the ramparts gave a yell of delight. But mostly, they were less frightened. A good round of brag almost always fortifies the heart.

"I'm an animal made of hard knocks," I kept a-boasting. "A horse that was never broke, a man of gumption, with bark on. I don't wear a collar round my neck, nor plow another man's furrow. I'm first-rate-and-a-half and a little past common. I'll stand up to the rack, fodder or no fodder. I am the yellow blossom of the gum swamp. And I wish that I may be shot if I do not go ahead to the very last. I shall never surrender or retreat!"

"Hurray for Crockett!" the men cried. "Hurray for Texas!"

To be truthful, I had given that same speech in Congress many times but to less effect. It warmed my heart to see 'em boys buck up.

Well, those Mexicans came at us starting before dawn on that thirteenth day, their trumpets blaring and their cannons roaring. Twice we beat 'em back, but finally they swarmed over the walls and put every last defender to the sword. But in the end, 'course, Texas prevailed. We lost the battle, but we won the war.

And that's how I became a legend. Where I am now, it's always springtime in the Smokies. And I have all day to roam and hunt and run with my dogs and politick with the varmints of the woods. At the end of the day, my pretty Polly is a-waiting in the cabin door with supper on the table and the youngsters round her skirts.

And I am eternally happy to be who I am, which is Davy Crockett, the original ring-tailed roarer of the western woods, the yellow blossom of the gum swamp.